TAHLEQUAH PUBLIC SCHOOLS
CENTRAL ELEMENTARY MEDIA CENTER

CHEROKEE ELEMENTARY
LIBRARY
TAHLEQUAH, OK
918-458-4110

Tahlequah Middle School Library
Tahlequah, OK

WOMEN EXPLORERS IN NORTH AND SOUTH AMERICA

NELLIE CASHMAN, VIOLET CRESSY-MARCKS, YNES MEXIA, MARY BLAIR NILES, ANNIE PECK

by Margo McLoone

Reading Consultant:
Dr. Patricia Gilmartin, Ph.D.
Professor of Geography
University of South Carolina

CAPSTONE PRESS
MANKATO, MINNESOTA

CAPSTONE PRESS
818 North Willow Street • Mankato, MN 56001

Copyright © 1997 Capstone Press. All rights reserved. No part of this book may be reproduced without written permission from the publisher.

Printed in the United States of America.

Library of Congress Cataloging-in-Publication Data
McLoone, Margo.
    Women explorers in North and South America: Nellie Cashman, Annie Peck, Ynes Mexia, Mary Blair Niles, Violet Cressy Marcks/by Margo McLoone.
        p. cm.--(Capstone short biographies)
    Includes bibliographical references and index.
    Summary: Summarizes the lives and accomplishments of five women who were explorers in North and South America.
    ISBN 1-56065-507-0
    1. Women explorers--America--Biography--Juvenile literature.
    2. America--Discovery and exploration--Juvenile literature.
    3. Women adventurers--America--Biography--Juvenile literature.
    [1. Explorers. 2. Women--Biography. 3. America--Discovery and exploration.]   I. Title. II. Series.
    E17.M44   1997
    910'.922--dc20
                                                96-43332
                                                CIP

Photo credits
Arizona Historical Society, 8 (neg. 1847), 12 (neg. 83A)
Jean Buldain, 45
FPG, 20; 36; Terry Molenaar, 6; Alan Bergman, 14
International Stock/Al Clayton, 43
Library of Congress, 34
Royal Geographic Society, London, 16 (neg. D2452)
Society of Woman Geographers, 30
Unicorn/David Shores, 4, 27
University of California-Berkeley, 22, 28
Visuals Unlimited/Jeff Greenberg, cover

TABLE OF CONTENTS

Chapter 1   What Is an Explorer? 5

Chapter 2   Nellie Cashman 9

Chapter 3   Violet Cressy-Marcks 17

Chapter 4   Ynes Mexia 23

Chapter 5   Mary Blair Niles 31

Chapter 6   Annie Peck 35

Chronology 40

Words to Know 42

To Learn More 44

Useful Addresses 46

Internet Sites 47

Index 48

CHAPTER 1

WHAT IS AN EXPLORER?

Explorers are people who want to learn about new and faraway places. They gather information about remote places and people. They usually write about their experiences, so others can learn.

Exploring versus Traveling

Explorers go places very few people have ever been. These lands are wild and sometimes dangerous. Often there are no hotels or restaurants. Sometimes there are no roads. Then explorers must find or build their own paths.

Explorers must find or build their own paths.

Explorers must be careful of meat-eating piranha fish that live in the Amazon.

Traveling is different than exploring. Travelers usually go places where there are other people. They stay in hotels and eat in restaurants.

Dangers Explorers Face

Explorers face many problems. The places they go are not on any maps. They use a compass. A compass tells them what direction they are going. But even with a compass, they can become lost.

Sometimes explorers climb high, icy mountains. Other explorers paddle down dangerous rivers. Sometimes they are attacked by wild animals. They cannot always find a hospital if they are hurt or sick.

Weather is also a danger. Blizzards, floods, or earthquakes can hurt explorers. It takes a long time for people to find and rescue a lost or injured explorer.

Explorers in North and South America

When people think about explorers, they usually think of men. But many women have explored unknown lands. They have made important discoveries.

This book tells about the lives and experiences of five women explorers. They left their homes for adventure. These women explored the wildernesses in North America and South America.

They explored places few people had ever been. Their experiences have helped people learn about the animals, land, and cultures of North America and South America.

CHAPTER 2

NELLIE CASHMAN 1850—1925

Nellie Cashman was born in Queenstown, Ireland, in 1850. Her family was too poor to buy food. She came to the United States with her mother and her sister, Fanny.

Cashman did not want to be poor again. She dreamed of making a lot of money and helping other people.

Living in the United States

In the 1860s, Cashman moved to Boston, Massachusetts. She was a bellhop in a hotel. A bellhop carries luggage to people's rooms.

> Nellie Cashman did not want to be poor again. She explored remote places to look for gold.

At that time, the American Civil War (1861-1865) was being fought. Ulysses S. Grant was a Union army general. He stayed at the hotel where Cashman worked.

Cashman told Grant about her dream to be rich. He told her that it was easier to make money in the West.

Angel of the Cassiar

In 1869, Cashman and her sister Fanny went west to San Francisco, California. Fanny married and settled down. Cashman did not. She went off to search for gold.

Cashman went to Nevada. She worked as a cook in several mining camps. She also learned how to prospect. Prospecting is searching for gold and other valuable minerals.

In 1877, Cashman went to the Cassiar, a wilderness region of British Columbia, Canada. She was the first white woman to explore the remote region.

Six other miners came with her. They found gold and staked a claim. Staking a claim means that they marked the place as their own. Then they left the claim to go home.

On their way home, they heard that miners were dying of scurvy. Scurvy is a disease caused by lack of vitamin C. Cashman and her partners wanted to help.

It was a dangerously cold winter. The snow was very deep. Wearing snowshoes, they pulled

heavy sleds loaded with food. It took them 77 days to reach the mining camp.

They gave potatoes to the sick men dying of scurvy. No one died after Cashman and her partners came with food. The miners called Cashman the Angel of the Cassiar.

Boom Town Days

Cashman moved to Tombstone, Arizona, in 1880. At that time, Tombstone was a fast-growing town called a boom town. Miners had found silver in the surrounding mountains.

Cashman opened a restaurant that served good, inexpensive food to miners. She gave free food to poor people.

Once, Cashman helped the sheriff stop an illegal hanging. The sheriff asked her to be a deputy, but she said no. She wanted to look for more gold.

To the Klondike

Gold was discovered in the Klondike territory of Canada in 1897. Cashman decided to go

---

Nellie Cashman spent her life helping others. Miners called her the Angel of the Cassiar.

Cashman journeyed on a dog sled to look for gold.

there to search for gold. She traveled the dangerous Skagway Trail to a mining town named Dawson.

Cashman explored the countryside to prospect for gold. She journeyed on snowshoes or on a dog sled. Once again, she struck it rich. She gave some of her money to poor people. The rest she used to explore and prospect.

To Alaska

Cashman followed the gold rush to Alaska. She stayed there for several years. She lived in an out-of-the-way place 60 miles (96 kilometers) north of the Arctic Circle. The Arctic Circle is the frozen area around the North Pole.

Cashman sailed wild rivers in handmade rafts. She survived blizzards without food or blankets.

At 70 years old, she made her last incredible journey. Cashman mushed, or drove a dog team 750 miles (1,200 kilometers). She made the trip over ice and snow. It took her 17 days.

Pictured on a Stamp

Cashman died of pneumonia in 1925. She was buried next to her sister, Fanny, in Victoria, British Columbia, Canada.

In 1984, Cashman was inducted into the Arizona Women's Hall of Fame. The United States Post Office honored her with a stamp. She was featured in a 1994 series called *Legends of the Old West*. Her stamp says, *Nellie Cashman, The Angel of Tombstone.*

CHAPTER 3

VIOLET CRESSY-MARCKS 1890—1970

Violet Rutley was born in England in 1890. She was the only daughter of William Rutley.

She married Captain Cressy-Marcks. They had a son and were divorced.

Across South America

Cressy-Marcks traveled across Scandinavia on a sled in 1929. The sled was pulled by reindeer. After that adventure, she wanted to keep

---

Violet Cressy-Marcks journeyed around the world eight times.

traveling. So she left for Brazil in 1930. At that time, Brazil was unexplored and unmapped.

Cressy-Marcks wanted to sail a boat up the Amazon river. Then she planned to take a mule over the Andes mountains. Finally, she wanted to take a train to Lima, Peru.

Cressy-Marcks was an experienced traveler. She listed the items she felt were basic for travel. The list included scientific instruments, revolvers, rifles, shotguns, cameras, a chair, a table, a canvas bath, cooking utensils, a medicine chest, and a tent.

Cressy-Marcks arrived in South America with a huge crate and many suitcases. Then she realized that she had brought too much. She sent most of it back to England.

Over the Andes Mountains

Cressy-Marcks was used to dangerous travel. But she still had problems in the Andes. She could not find food, mules, or guides.

Her problems continued. A snake bit her leg. The wound became infected, and she had trouble walking. She burned her clothes when

Cressy-Marcks studied the ruins of Machu Piccu.

drying them over a fire. She was left with only a nightgown and a pair of shoes to wear.

Cressy-Marcks hiked part of the way over the Andes. She became very cold and sick. Luckily, two other travelers saw her. They agreed to take her to a city by mule. To get to the city, they rode through a dangerous snowstorm.

Finally, they reached a city. Cressy-Marcks immediately checked into a fancy hotel to recover from her journey. She hired a bus for the rest of her trip.

Cressy-Marcks journeyed to other remote places like Machu Piccu and Lake Titicaca. She wrote the book *Up the Amazon and Over the Andes*. It is about her adventures in South America.

After South America

Cressy-Marcks went on to travel around the world eight times. She hunted big game animals, such as elephants and bears. She studied the remains of ancient civilizations.

Cressy-Marcks took photographs and made movies of her explorations. She talked and wrote about what she learned. She died on September 10, 1970.

CHAPTER 4

YNES MEXIA
1870—1938

Ynes Mexia was born in Washington, D.C., on May 24, 1870. Because her father was a diplomat from Mexico, her family lived in the United States. Diplomats are people who represent their country's government in a foreign country.

Her parents were divorced when Mexia was nine years old. She moved to Philadelphia, Pennsylvania, to live with her mother. She grew up in the United States.

Later, she moved to Mexico to care for her father who was ill. He died in 1896. Mexia married twice while living in Mexico. Her first

Ynes Mexia explored the wilderness to collect rare plants.

husband died. She divorced her second husband, and then returned to the United States.

Adventuring Alone
Mexia had become physically and emotionally ill in Mexico. She moved to San Francisco, California, to receive help from a doctor. She recovered and began to hike in the woods.

She became interested in botany, which is the study of plants. She explored the wilderness to collect rare plants.

Soul of an Explorer
Mexia spent 13 years exploring Mexico and South America. She preferred being alone to gather plants from jungles and mountains.

A fellow collector said Mexia had an explorer's soul. She was happiest when she was far away from cities and other people.

Up the Amazon River
In 1929, Mexia collected plants in Brazil for several months. She sent her collection of samples back to the United States.

Mexia decided to take a trip up the Amazon river. It was her dream journey. She used a river steamer, riverboat, and canoe to journey up the Amazon. She covered 3,000 miles (4,800 kilometers). She went all the way to its source in the Andes mountains of Peru. The source is the point where a river begins.

Piranhas

Mexia had to be careful of piranha fish on her journey up the Amazon. Piranha live in the Amazon.
 Piranhas have razor-sharp teeth. They can chew off a person's leg in less than one minute.

Mexia hired a guide and three men to paddle the canoe. They passed through the Pongo de Manseriche. This is known as the Iron Gate of the Upper Amazon. It is a seven-mile (11-kilometer) stretch of river that flows through a deep gorge. A gorge is a narrow passage through steep walls of earth or rock. Very few outsiders had seen the Pongo.

With the Araguarunas

For three months, Mexia lived on the land of the Araguarunas (ah-RAH-gwah-roo-nahs). The Araguarunas are an Amazon Indian tribe. Mexia ate roots, roasted monkeys, and parrots.

Mexia journeyed up the Amazon in a canoe.

    The Araguarunas believed that their enemies caused sickness and death. They were headhunters. A headhunter is a person who cuts off an enemy's head. Then the head is dried, preserved, and shrunk. The Araguarunas

believed that the dried heads would keep evil spirits away.

Mexia became friends with the Araguaranas. They built a special raft for her to travel back down the Amazon.

A Home for Her Collection

Mexia explored for two more years. Then she went back to Mexico. She spent her time in Mexico collecting plant samples. On July 12, 1938, Mexia died.

Mexia had a large collection of South American pottery and artifacts. Artifacts are objects created by humans. Artifacts are usually used for a practical purpose. Her collection was donated to the University of California.

Mexia's plant samples are on display all over the world. She discovered more than 500 new kinds of plants. Some of these were named after her.

Mexia discovered more than 500 new kinds of plants.

CHAPTER 5

MARY BLAIR NILES 1880—1959

Mary Blair Rice was born in Coles Ferry, Virginia, on June 15, 1880. She used Blair as a first name. She married William Beebe in 1902.

William worked for the New York Zoological Society. He studied birds. Together, Blair and William explored the world to find rare birds. William wanted to study the birds in their natural habitat. A habitat is the place where something normally lives and grows.

The Society of Woman Geographers gave Mary Blair Niles a special award for her explorations.

For 10 years, the Beebes searched South America, Mexico, and the Far East. Then they were divorced. Afterwards, Blair met and married a photographer named Robert Niles.

To Devil's Island

Together, Blair and Robert Niles explored Ecuador, Colombia, Haiti, Guatemala, French Guiana, and Peru. She went to remote towns and talked with local people. Robert photographed the people and the wild scenery.

Blair studied the history and literature of South America. She wrote books. Her books combined her travel experiences and Robert's photographs.

The most exciting trip they took was to Devil's Island. The island was a penal colony in French Guiana. A penal colony is a place where prisoners are sent to live as a punishment. Blair was the first foreign woman to visit Devil's Island.

Accomplishments

Blair wrote about the cruel treatment prisoners received on the jungle island. Her story and

Robert's photographs shocked the world. The French government closed the prison.

Blair wrote the book *A Journey in Time: Peruvian Pageant*. The city of Lima, Peru, awarded her a gold medal for her book in 1938.

The Society of Woman Geographers in Washington, D.C., gave her a special award for her explorations in 1944. Blair Niles died in New York on April 13, 1959.

CHAPTER 6

ANNIE PECK
1850—1935

Annie Peck was born in Providence, Rhode Island, on October 19, 1850. Peck was one of the first women to become a college professor.

Peck took a trip to Switzerland in 1885. There she saw a mountain known as the Matterhorn. She promised herself that someday she would climb it.

To practice, she climbed mountains in California, New England, Mexico, and Europe. She gave up teaching to climb mountains.

Peck became the third woman to climb the Matterhorn in 1895. Her climb made her a

Annie Peck gave up teaching to climb mountains.

world-famous mountain climber. People were shocked because she wore pants to climb mountains. At that time, women were expected to wear floor-length skirts or dresses.

Climbing Mount Huascaran

Peck's next plan was to climb Mount Huascaran in the Andes mountains of Peru. It is the highest mountain in North and South America. It rises more than 22,000 feet (6,600 meters) above sea level. Sea level is the average level of the surface of the ocean.

Peck tried to climb Mount Huascaran five times over four years. She suffered from frostbite, windburn, and sunburn. She went without food for so long that she almost starved. She crossed dangerous ice bridges and climbed snowy glaciers. Once, one of her companions became mentally unstable. He hid some of Peck's equipment. She never found it.

The higher Peck climbed, the harder it was for her to breathe. The air is thinner at higher

People were shocked that Peck wore pants and not dresses to climb mountains.

altitudes. Altitudes are measured by how high above sea level one is.

Peck had been turned back by avalanches, guides who left her, and lost equipment. Finally, she reached the top of Mount Huascaran in 1908. But then she had to go back down the mountain.

It was cold, dark, and slippery. She was tired and hungry. She was worried that she might not make it back alive. But she wanted the world to know about her success.

Peck lost a mitten. Her hand kept freezing. But that did not stop her. Her strong will helped her make it back down the mountain.

Exploring by Air

From 1929 to 1930, Peck was a passenger in dozens of airplanes that flew over South America. She photographed the places she explored. She wrote guidebooks for travelers.

Peck wrote about climbing Mount Huascaran in *A Search for the Apex of America*. She also wrote, *Flying over South America: Twenty Thousand Miles by Air*. In

1928, the Lima Geographic Society named the north peak of Mount Huascaran Ana Peck Peak to honor her.

Peck was a member of the Society of Woman Geographers and Great Britain's Royal Geographic Society. Peck died on July 18, 1935. She was 84 years old.

CHRONOLOGY

Nellie Cashman

1850
Born in Queenstown, Ireland

1860s
Immigrates to United States; works as a bellhop in Boston

1869
Moves to San Francisco, California

1877
Journeys to Canada to search for gold

1880
Moves to Tombstone, Arizona, to look for silver

1925
Dies of pneumonia in Canada

Annie Peck

1850
Born in Providence, Rhode Island

1895
Climbs the Matterhorn in the Alpine Mountain Range

1908
Climbs Mount Huascaran in the Andes mountains

1929
Travels in airplanes over South America

1935
Dies on July 18

Ynes Mexia

1870
Born in Washington, D.C.

1890s
Moves to Mexico to nurse her father

1896
Father dies in Mexico

1929
Collects plants in Brazil; goes on journey up the Amazon river and to its source

1938
Dies on July 12 in Mexico

Mary Blair Niles

1880
Born in Coles Ferry, Virginia

1902—1912
Explores South America, Mexico, and Far East

1938
Receives gold medal from the city of Lima, Peru, for her book *A Journey in Time: Peruvian Pageant*

1944
Receives special award from Society of Woman Geographers

1959
Dies in New York

Violet Cressy-Marcks

1890
Born in England

1929
Travels across Scandinavia in a sled

1930
Explores Brazil

1970
Dies on September 10

WORDS TO KNOW

claim (KLAYM)—to say something belongs to you; in this case, a portion of land used for mining
gorge (GORJ)—a deep, narrow passage with steep, rocky sides
habitat (HAB-uh-tat)—the place and natural conditions in which something normally lives
headhunter (hed-HUHN-tur)—someone who kills enemies and cuts off their heads, then preserves, shrinks, and keeps them to ward off evil spirits
mush (MUHSH)—to travel over snow with a dog sled
penal colony (PEE-nuhl KOL-uh-nee)—a place where prisoners are forced to live as a punishment for their crimes
prospect (PROSS-pekt)—to search for gold or other valuable minerals

Sometimes Amazon Indians helped explorers.

scurvy (SKUR-vee)—a disease caused by lack of vitamin C

TO LEARN MORE

Cooper, Kay. *Where In the World Are You?* New York: Walker, 1990.

National Geographic Society. *Exploring Your World: The Adventure of Geography.* Washington, D.C.: National Geographic Society, 1989.

Lourie, Peter. *Amazon.* Honesdale, Penn.: Caroline House, 1991.

Matthews, Rupert. *Explorer.* London: Dorling Kindersley, 1991.

Rappaport, Doreen. *Living Dangerously: American Women Who Risked Their Lives for Adventure.* New York: HarperCollins, 1991.

Explorers in North and South America had to journey through waterfalls and rapids.

USEFUL ADDRESSES

Information Center on Children's Cultures
332 East 38th Street
New York, NY 10016

National Geographic Society
1145 17th Street NW
Washington, DC 20036-4688

Royal Canadian Geographic Association
39 McArthur Avenue
Vanier, ON K1L 8L7
Canada

Society of Woman Geographers
415 East Capitol Street
Washington, DC 20003

INTERNET SITES

Earthwatch
http://www.earthwatch.org

The Explorers' Club
http://caldera.wr.usgs.gov/mdiggles/EC.html

GlobaLearn
http://www.globalearn.org

Mountain Travel Sobek: Adventure Company
http://www.mtsobek.com/

National Geographic Society
http://www.nationalgeographic.com/main.wd

INDEX

Alaska, 15
Amazon, 19, 21, 26, 29
Andes, 21, 26, 37
Araguarunas, 26, 27, 29
Arctic Circle, 15
Arizona Women's Hall of Fame, 15

Boston, Massachusetts, 9
botany, 25
Brazil, 19, 25

California, 10, 25, 29
Canada, 10, 13, 15
Cashman, Nellie, 9-11, 13-15
Cassiar, 10, 13
Cressy-Marcks, Violet, 17, 19-21

Dawson, Canada, 14
Devil's Island, 32

French Guiana, 32

Grant, Ulysses S., 10

headhunters, 27

Ireland, 9

Klondike, 13

Lake Titicaca, 21

Machu Piccu, 21
Matterhorn, 35
Mexia, Ynes, 23, 25, 26, 29
Mexico, 23, 25, 29
Mount Huascaran, 37, 38, 39

Niles, Mary Blair, 31-33

Peck, Annie, 35, 37-39
Peru, 19, 26, 32, 33, 37
prospect, 10, 14

Royal Geographic Society, 39

Scandanavia, 17
scurvy, 11, 13
Skagway Trail, 14
Society of Woman Geographers, 33, 39

Tombstone, Arizona, 13, 15

TAHLEQUAH PUBLIC SCHOOLS
ELEMENTARY MEDIA CENTER

920   McLoone, Margo
MCL   Women explorers in
         North and South
         America

Tahlequah Middle School Library
Tahlequah, OK